Buttercup Sunshine AND THE Zombies OF Dooooom

For Matthew,
who loved to laugh.

Buttercup Sunshine

AND THE

Zombies

OF

DOOoOOM

Buttercup Sunshine and the Zombies of Dooooom
An original concept by author Colin Mulhern
© Colin Mulhern

Illustrations by Colin Mulhern
Cover artwork © Risa Rodil

Published by MAVERICK ARTS PUBLISHING LTD
Studio 3a, City Business Centre, 6 Brighton Road,
Horsham, West Sussex, RH13 5BB
+44 (0) 1403 256941
© Maverick Arts Publishing Limited September 2018

A CIP catalogue record for this book is available
at the British Library.

ISBN: 978-1-84886-330-9

CHAPTER ONE

Granny Fondant lived in a small, white house with a roof made from straw and window boxes bursting with colour. A window poked out through the roof, a short chimney was plonked on top and sunflowers grew in the garden. In short, this little house couldn't have looked more like the perfect storybook cottage unless it had been made from gingerbread.

Granny Fondant rose early and opened the windows. The sky was blue, birdsong filled the air and everything was just right for another perfect day in Briar's Cove – the nicest, safest, sweetest town there ever was, where nothing bad ever happened.

In the distance, she could see a figure running down Honeysuckle Lane. It was a little girl. She had a lemon dress as bright as the sun and the bow in her hair bounced as she ran. Granny recognised her immediately as Buttercup Sunshine - the friendliest, most angelic little girl you

could ever imagine.

'Good morning, Buttercup!' called Granny, waving a hand.

Buttercup didn't wave back. This was mostly due to the fact that she was carrying something. It was a big, heavy something – bright red, with a large handle.

Granny Fondant had to adjust her glasses to check she wasn't seeing things. How odd. Why would Buttercup be holding a chainsaw?

Granny's smile began to fade, because there was something else odd. Buttercup was usually smiling or laughing when she came skipping down Honeysuckle lane, not running at full pelt with her eyes wide and screaming, 'Grannneeeeee! Shut your window!'

Granny Fondant blinked. 'Buttercup?'

The little girl kicked open the gate, raced up the garden path and burst in through the front door.

'Granny?' she panted.

8

'Granny?' She took a moment to catch her breath. 'Have you got any petrol?'

'Petrol? Whatever for? I don't even own a car. No, of course I don't have petrol.'

Buttercup staggered into the front room. She dumped the chainsaw on the floor with a metallic clunk. 'Well, I guess that thing's useless then.' She stepped back into the hallway. 'We need to lock the front door.'

'Lock the door?' Granny Fondant frowned.

'No one ever locks their doors in Briar's Cove.

Why, this is the nicest, safest, sweetest place there ever was, where nothing bad ever happens. We're famous for it.'

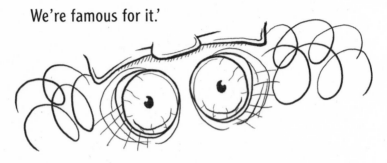

Buttercup's eyes were very nearly bursting with horror. 'Things have changed, Granny. We need to jam this door shut. And the same with the windows.' She looked about, as if searching the room for something. 'Have you got anything we can use as weapons?'

Granny held up her hands. 'Now just hold your

horses, young lady. Dear me, I knew you had a good imagination, but my word. Just look at you! What is that mess all over your dress?' Then she paused, her face suddenly brightening up.

'Ohh,' she said. 'That rhymes. Did you hear, Buttercup? That mess on your dress. Granny made a rhyme. I'll write it down.'

'Granny, stop!' cried Buttercup. 'Things aren't fine, and there's no time for a rhyme.' She grabbed Granny by the arm.

'We're in **DANGER**, Granny.'

Granny pulled away. 'Nonsense. There's no danger here. You know very well that this is the nicest, safest-'

'No, Granny. Not anymore. Something...' Buttercup paused, trying to find a word that would get her message across. 'Something really **BAD** has happened.'

There was the sudden sound of a needle scratching across a vinyl record and Granny gasped. Had she been holding a cup, she'd have dropped it. Had she been playing darts, she'd have completely missed the board.

In little more than a whisper, Granny stammered, 'B-b-bad? No... It's a mistake. It can't be true. Nothing bad ever happens in Briar's Cove. You're being silly. This is another of your games, isn't it dear?'

Buttercup grabbed a chair and wedged it against the front door.

'It's no game, Granny,' she said. 'Even I couldn't make this up. And if we don't find a way to lock those windows, things are going to get a lot worse.' She ran back to the front room and looked out at

Honeysuckle Lane. 'They'll be here any minute.'

'Who? What is going on, Buttercup? Tell me. Tell me, right now.'

With a shaking finger, Buttercup pointed. 'That's who. Right there.'

Granny Fondant looked to where the little girl was pointing. At the farthest point of Honeysuckle Lane there was a wall of shambling figures, their arms were stretched out and they were swaying this way and that as they scraped their feet, step by agonising step, towards the cottage.

Granny adjusted her spectacles. 'What in the world...?'

'ZOMBIES,' whispered Buttercup. 'And they're coming to get us.'

'Zombies?' muttered Granny. She looked lost, like she couldn't quite believe this was happening. 'But... but how?'

'It doesn't matter how. What matters is stopping them. We need to stop them, Granny, and we need to do it now.'

'Why? What in the world do these zombies want?'

'Want?' Buttercup's eyes flicked nervously towards the windows. Then she hissed, 'Brains.'

'Brains?'

'That's right, Granny. It's our *brains* they're after. They want to eat our brains.'

dinner

CHAPTER TWO

Buttercup was in a whirl, opening and closing the windows to see if they would lock.

Granny Fondant sat in her chair looking slightly confused at the presence of a chainsaw in the middle of the carpet.

'Buttercup?' she asked carefully. 'Where did you get a chainsaw?'

Buttercup called over her shoulder, 'I found it.' She gave the window another hard slam. 'I think we're going to have to nail the windows shut. It's the only solution.'

But Granny was still looking at the heavy-duty power tool with a certain air of suspicion. In particular, the splatters of green streaked across the red metal body.

'You don't simply *find* a chainsaw. It isn't like a dandelion or a ladybird.'

'It doesn't matter where I got it. We need to get the windows locked tight.'

Granny was scratching the fine grey hairs that grew on her chin. 'I've found many things in my time. Coins, gloves, mismatched socks. Things like that. I don't think I've ever found a chainsaw.'

'Okay, then. I borrowed it. From a lumberjack.'

'A lumberjack? The only lumberjack I know is Mr Blackberry.'

'That's him. He lives in the Wicked Woods of Woe.'

Granny frowned.

'The Wicked Woods of What?'

'Of Woe.'

Granny frowned for a moment then smiled. 'Oh, I think you mean the Wicked Woods of Wooaahhhh. I haven't seen Mr Blackberry in ages. I wonder how he is these days.'

Buttercup looked round at Granny. 'Not terribly well. He's undead.'

'*Un*-dead?'

'He's a zombie, Granny. He's just like the rest of them. It's a bit of a long story, but the short version is that he's on his way with the rest of them.' Buttercup looked out through the window. 'In fact, I can see him now. He's right there at the front, and he's leading them right here.'

It was true. The wall of zombies was steadily moving closer to the cottage, and right at the front of them was one taller than the rest. Even from this distance it was possible to

Bite mark

Sunken eyes

No smile

Zombie hands

see that his skin wasn't quite as decayed and his clothes weren't the rotting rags worn by the others. In fact, his red checked shirt – the international uniform of the lumberjack – was clear to see.

'Oh my,' said Granny. 'He doesn't look well at all.'

'No, he doesn't,' said Buttercup, 'and if he gets here before we lock the doors and windows, we're going to look exactly the same.'

Granny Fondant stepped back. 'Close the curtains, dear. If they don't see us, they'll think no one's home. Perhaps they'll go straight past.'

'I don't think so. They're drawn by the smell. That's how they followed me. They can smell our brains, Granny. They won't stop until they get their teeth in them.'

Granny put a hand to her mouth and thought for a moment. Then she clicked her fingers. 'I know,' she said.

'Yes?'

'I'll put the kettle on.'

'How will that help?'

Granny looked out at the wall of groaning, staggering figures and said, 'Well, they're walking quite slowly. It'll be a while before they get here. That should be enough time for you to tell me how this strange affair all came about.'

Buttercup gaped. Her mouth actually dropped. The hordes of the undead were on their way and very soon they would be shambling up the garden path and hammering on the front door.

On the other hand, she'd done a lot of running that morning and a cup of tea sounded like a pretty good idea.

'Got any biscuits?'

Granny filled the kettle. 'I made shortbread only this morning.' She wiped her hands on her frilly lined apron and said, 'Now then, what happened exactly?'

Buttercup flopped down onto the chair.

'It all began...

...with **A STAR...**'

27

CHAPTER THREE

Buttercup had been investigating a crime. It was late and it was dark, but it always made sense to Buttercup to investigate crimes in the dark because her torch had a better effect at night time. She could sweep the beam this way and that, casting shadows here and there.

The crime for this particular night was a missing thimble.

At some point, a thief had broken into the sewing kit, stolen the thimble and had hidden it somewhere in the garden. The only evidence was the open sewing kit on Buttercup's bedroom floor and the catapult she had used... sorry, the catapult the mysterious thief had used to fire the thimble into the bushes.

In order to crack the crime, Buttercup needed two things: a high power torch to see in the dark and a micro walkie-talkie to stay in touch with her partner.

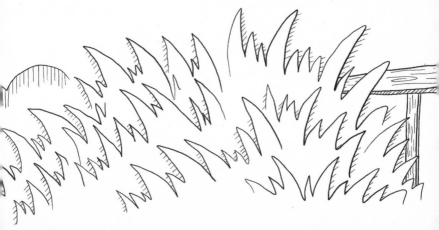

She hooked one walkie-talkie over her ear and placed the other one down next to Barry.

'There you go, Barry,' she said. 'And stay sharp, this could turn nasty.'

Barry said nothing. This was because Barry was a small brown toad who lived by the pond in the garden. Barry was nocturnal, which meant he only came out at night. He would crawl out, sit on the edge of the pond and croak. He didn't do a lot more.

But to Buttercup, Barry was in the control centre. He was logged onto a super-computer and could hack into any system. He was her eyes and ears and those croaks weren't just the soggy ramblings of a mere toad. Those croaks were warnings, and each time Barry made a noise, Buttercup would press her fingers to the earpiece and reply with, 'that's a ten-four,' or 'copy that!' and continue on her mission.

At the bottom of the garden, Buttercup swept her torchlight across the hedge. 'Barry, I need a situation update ASAP.'

Croak.

Buttercup translated the croak into an American accent: 'That's gonna take some time, Agent Sunshine.'

She switched back to her own voice. 'No, Barry. I need it now!' She looked under the hedge. No signs of the thimble, but there was a sudden shuffle in the leaves up ahead.

Buttercup bent low and shone her torch into the darkness below the hedge. And there, in the shadows, a small hedgehog shuffled away from the light.

Buttercup pressed her hand to her ear and kept her voice low. 'Barry, are you getting this? I'm in a flank-two position. Tango spotted.' She crept back, away from the hedge and shone her torch at the garden gate. 'I'm going to attack from the north side. Stay with me.'

In a sudden burst of movement, Buttercup ran at the gate, leapt into the air and...

Her foot caught on the top of the gate.

Any other girl would have splattered on her face, but not Buttercup. Instinctively, she let go of the torch, reached out towards the ground and landed in a tight roll.

The torch clattered to the side and went out.

Darkness.

Silence.

Still in character, Buttercup lay on her back. 'I've been hit, Barry. Send an EVAC team and...' She stopped.

There was something up above, something moving in the night sky.

She frowned. 'What in the world is that?'

Slowly, she got to her feet, still looking at the stars above. There was one that was larger and brighter than all the rest. It appeared to be sailing across the heavens with a strange smudge of green mist behind it.

'Are you seeing this, Barry?'

Through her earpiece, Buttercup heard the telltale

plop of Barry slipping into the pond – a sign

that his involvement in the game was over. He'd

probably be at the bottom of the pond for the rest

of the night, but that didn't stop Buttercup's

investigation. She put a hand to her ear and her

partner's voice came through loud and clear. 'I've

switched to sub-aquatic communication,

Buttercup. Hardware is ready for pick-up.'

Buttercup grabbed the torch. 'That's a ten-four,

Barry.' She skipped back to the pond and retrieved

the spare earpiece. 'Hardware collected.'

She looked again at the star.

'There's something very strange up there.'

'Treat the situation with extreme caution, Agent Sunshine.'

Buttercup blinked. That star was bigger! In the space of just a few seconds, the star actually looked brighter and greener too. In fact, even as she watched, it looked…

WHOOSH!

In a streak of green light, the star came hurtling down like a rocket. It seemed to disappear behind distant trees and a moment later, a huge flash illuminated the entire sky.

'A meteorite!' cried Buttercup. 'Stars don't go falling to earth and exploding like that. That's a meteorite from outer space.'

She jumped up onto the gatepost and tried to see where it had landed. The flash had died but there was still a green glow in the sky, cutting the line of trees into black, jagged teeth.

'It landed in the forest,' she whispered. 'In the Wicked Woods of Woe.'

Just by her feet, the hedgehog came out from its hiding place. Buttercup looked down at the small, spiky creature and said, 'If that's a meteorite, there might be a piece of space rock for me to find. It could be valuable. It could be made entirely of diamonds. I could end up rich.'

She looked at the glow above the trees. 'First thing in the morning, I'm heading off to find exactly where that thing landed.'

The hedgehog shuffled a little closer.

Buttercup looked down at the hedgehog. 'What's that?'

The hedgehog, of course, said nothing.

Buttercup's eyes widened. 'You think I should go now?' She looked back at the trees. 'You're right, hedgehog. That's what any brave girl worth her salt would do. There's no time to lose.'

She shot into the house and came back a moment later with a map. She clicked on the torch, examined the map and looked out at the glow in the distance. 'If my calculations are correct...' She stabbed the map with a finger. 'The comet will

have landed right there!' She glanced back at the
pond. 'Barry. Keep all systems on standby.'

Buttercup opened the gate.

'But for now,' she said. 'I'm on my own.'

CHAPTER FOUR

'Where did it land?' asked Granny.

Buttercup checked the window for zombies. They were still a good way off.

'In a cemetery,' she said, sitting back down. 'Right in the middle of the Wicked Woods of Woe.'

'A cemetery?' asked Granny. 'In the Wicked Woods

of Wooaahhhh? Are you sure?'

Buttercup handed Granny Fondant the map, pointing to an area in the deepest, darkest part of the forest. 'Right there,' she said. 'It's called the Forgotten Cemetery.'

Granny adjusted her spectacles. 'Oh yes. I'd forgotten about that.' Then she looked up. 'But surely, you didn't go there? Not in the dark?'

'There was no time to lose, Granny. Besides, I had a torch. It was only a creepy old forest at night. What could possibly go wrong?'

'So what happened?'

'It all went wrong.'

*

The light of Buttercup's torch flashed through the darkness of the forest, illuminating the folds and wrinkles in the bark of ancient trees. The shadows moved and twisted. The branches overhead clawed together like the fingers of some skeletal trap. Any ordinary girl would have been reduced to a quivering mass of jelly, if not for the trees and their terrible shapes then definitely for the noises that called out from the shadows: the hoot of a

lonely owl, something slithering in the undergrowth, and what was that? The distant howl of a wolf?

It was difficult to make out due to another noise. A kind of rasping roar that got louder the deeper she ventured into the forest.

Buttercup put a hand to her ear. 'Barry? Are you picking this up? It sounds like some kind of engine.' She tried to feel her way through branches that brushed and scratched at her arms. A little further along, she could make out a chink of light up ahead. Not the green light she was hoping for, but an orange, flickering light. And the closer she got

Orange Glow

to the light, the louder the rasping roar became.

'What in the world is that noise? It sounds like a drill. Or maybe a washing machine full of pebbles on a super high spin.'

Barry was unusually quiet, possibly because the light up ahead had Buttercup's full attention. She pushed on, creeping closer and closer.

Finally, she realised that the light up ahead was a bonfire, burning in the centre of a small clearing. The orange light lit up the surrounding trees as well as a wooden hut at the far side. At this side, however, a monstrous beast was cast into silhouette against the orange glow. A huge, humanoid shape, its arms raised high above its head, holding up the machine that was making all the noise.

Buttercup flashed her torch on the creature and it immediately whirled around.

It was a man. He had appeared as big as a bear against the firelight, but now Buttercup could see that he was wearing several padded shirts. And the machine he was holding, the thing that had made all of that noise, was in fact, a huge red chainsaw.

'What the...?' The man screamed and stepped back, squinting his eyes at the beam of light from the torch. 'Who's that? Who's there?'

Buttercup's mouth dropped. 'Mr Blackberry?' She lowered the beam of the torch and stepped forward. 'It's only me. Buttercup Sunshine.'

'Buttercup?' Mr Blackberry's eyes looked ready to pop. 'All the way from Briar's Cove?'

The chainsaw coughed and spluttered and as the engine

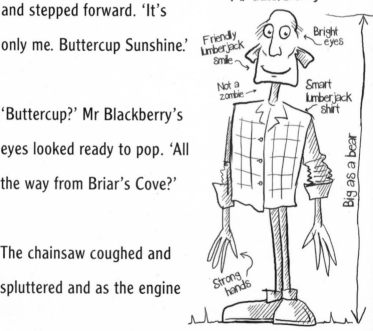

Mr Blackberry

Friendly lumberjack smile

Bright eyes

Not a zombie

Smart lumberjack shirt

Big as a bear

Strong hands

stopped, Mr Blackberry groaned, 'Ah, not again.'
He dumped the thing on the ground and wiped his
hands on his shirt. 'What on earth are you doing
creeping around a forest in the middle of the
night?'

Buttercup answered him right back, 'What are *you*
doing chopping up logs in the middle of the night?'

'I'm nocturnal, that's what.'

'Nocturnal?'

'Yeah, you know, like bats and owls and foxes.'

'And toads and hedgehogs?'

'Yes. And pretty much every other animal in this forest. I'm like them, I am. I only come out at night.'

'Since when?'

Mr Blackberry picked up a small log and stepped towards the fire. 'Thursday.'

Buttercup followed. 'Why?'

The lumberjack dumped the log in the flames and turned to face Buttercup.

'Have you ever tried to get a good night's sleep in the middle of a forest?' he asked. 'Oh, it's lovely and peaceful during the day. That's because everything's asleep. But at night, the whole bloomin' place wakes up. I got sick of lying in my bed, wide awake because of all those HOOTS and GROWLS and SQUEAKS. So I thought, if you can't beat 'em, join 'em. I got up, got dressed and set to work. I sleep during the day now and I chop trees at night.'

'Is that better?'

'Not really. Can't see a thing most of the time. Nearly sawed my thumb off just before you turned up.' He blinked and wiped his brow with a sleeve. 'So come on then, what's your excuse, Buttercup Sunshine? What are you doing out here? A little girl like you should be in bed.'

'Did you see the meteorite?'

'Do you mean that bright green flash that went shooting through the sky? It seemed to land just over that way, through those trees. There was a huge BANG, and the ground shook so hard I thought half these trees would collapse.'

'Didn't you investigate?'

Mr Blackberry's face darkened. 'Oh, I don't go over that way, little Miss. And I don't advise you to go either. There's a darkness over there...' he paused, then added, 'Well not so much tonight as there's more of a green glow, but generally speaking there's a darkness and a sense of evil in the air. That's not a part of the forest I like to go to.'

Buttercup checked her map. 'It says on here there's a cemetery.'

'That's right,' said the lumberjack.

'They call it the Forgotten Cemetery, and it was left forgotten for a reason.'

'What reason?'

Mr Blackberry shrugged. 'No one can remember, but some things are best forgotten, little Miss. I don't believe in ghosts and ghoulies and the like, but I do believe that some things should simply be left alone.'

'But there could be space rock, and it might be valuable. Imagine if the meteorite was made of

DIAMONDS.'

'Diamonds, you say?' Mr Blackberry frowned. 'Well, I suppose it wouldn't hurt just to have a small look, just to check it out. I could do with a new chainsaw. That one uses up petrol in five minutes flat.'

'Then let's go and find us some space-treasure, Mr Blackberry.' Buttercup shone the light of her torch towards the green glow coming through the trees.

'I've got the torch, so I'll lead the way.'

Green Glow

CHAPTER FIVE

And so, with Buttercup shining her torch into the gloom, they followed a narrow trail that cut through the trees. Deeper and deeper into the forest they went, where the sounds of unseen predators hiding in the undergrowth were even louder, as were the death squawks of their prey.

'It can't be much further,' said Buttercup. 'The light is getting brighter.'

And it was. A bright, green glow filtered through the mist that seemed to pour from the area up ahead, a mist that grew so thick that Buttercup could no longer see her own feet.

Just up ahead, where the light was even brighter, a set of rusty and buckled iron gates rose up out of the mist.

'They must be the gates to the cemetery,' she whispered. 'But why is there no path?'

'There was once,' said Mr Blackberry. 'But it's almost completely gone now. Overgrown. And look how the trees have crept right up to the wall.'

Buttercup could barely follow the crumbling line of the dry, stone wall for the vines and leaves which crawled over every rock and into every crack and crevice. But this was no time to take in the scenery – Buttercup had investigating to do.

As they walked inside the cemetery gates, they both looked up at the ruins of an ancient church, standing tall against the moonlit sky. This alone would normally have a creep-factor of 8 or 9, but with the green glow illuminating the front, it looked like

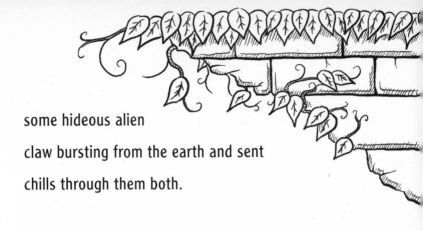

some hideous alien
claw bursting from the earth and sent
chills through them both.

Buttercup looked about the landscape of the
graveyard. The mist swirled and flowed around the
headstones, and there, right in the middle of the
cemetery where the light was brightest, was a huge
open pit.

'The meteorite must have landed right there,' said
Buttercup. She stepped towards the crater but as
she got closer she realised that the green glow
wasn't only coming from the pit – it was seeping
through countless cracks and gaps in the ground,
poking up through the long grass and putting the

worn names on the headstones into dark relief.

'What's that sound?' asked Mr Blackberry.

Buttercup paused to listen. The sound he was talking about was like a distant, muffled moan, coupled with knocks and bangs and rattles.

'It seems to be coming from the pit,' said Mr Blackberry.

Buttercup stood stone still as she tried to locate the source of the sounds. 'It's not coming from the pit,' she said. 'It's coming from the graves. It sounds like there are people down there. It sounds like people moaning and knocking on wood.'

'Well that doesn't make sense,' said Mr Blackberry. 'There's nothing down there but dead bodies. This is a graveyard. They hardly ever bury living people. I think there's a law against that.'

Buttercup looked at the mist pouring from the pit. 'It must be something to do with the meteorite,' she said. 'That green light must have some strange, alien quality. Look at the mist. Look how it's seeping through the ground.'

Again, the moans and the bangs below, and the scraping of fingernails on wood.

Carefully, Buttercup took a step back and looked at Mr Blackberry. 'I think it's brought them back to life.'

'Back to life?' Mr Blackberry was horrified. 'Then we must save them. Those poor people will be trapped. We need to find a shovel.'

Buttercup took another step back and shone her torch at the ground below. 'There's no need for a shovel, Mr Blackberry. Look!'

All around the graveyard, wherever the green light shone through, the earth appeared to be moving. In some places fingers were poking through, in others, hands were clawing at the surface, scraping the soil away. A second later, heads became visible. Then shoulders…

THE BODIES OF THE DEAD WERE CRAWLING THEIR WAY TO THE SURFACE.

CHAPTER SIX

'It's a miracle,' said Mr Blackberry. 'The meteorite must have some ultra magical properties and has somehow cured them of being dead.'

Buttercup turned the beam of her torch onto the nearest night crawler. Beneath the streaks of mud and dirt, the skin was a deep and muddy dark green. It was also hanging off in torn flaps and chunks. As the figure crawled further out, she saw how it sniffed the air. Its eyes locked on hers and it sniffed again.

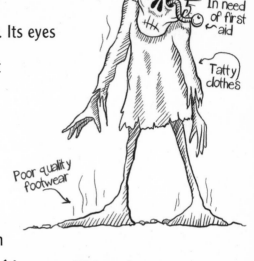

In a voice that was little more than a choke, the thing from the grave called out, 'Huuungrry...'

Buttercup wrinkled her nose at the stench of the thing at her feet. 'I'm not so sure they're cured,' she said. 'There's a name for people who come crawling out of their graves like that.'

'Well, according to the headstone,' said Mr

Blackberry, 'this one is called Arthur.'

'I don't mean that.'

'Huuungrry,' the thing at her feet muttered, and pulled itself a little closer to her.

'Only last week, Miss Morbid handed out loads of pamphlets. Little booklets on all kinds of horrible things, and one of them was all about what we're seeing right now.' Buttercup shuffled back from the creature at her feet. 'Those aren't people, Mr Blackberry. I think they're zombies.'

She expected Mr Blackberry to reply in shock and terror. Something along the lines of, 'Zombies? Quick, let's run away.' Or perhaps denial, like 'Zombies? There's no such thing.' What she certainly didn't expect was to have Mr Blackberry completely ignore her, lean down to the nearest living corpse and say, 'Come on then, Arthur. Let me help you out.'

The very next moment, he had his arms under the zombie's armpits and was heaving the old guy up. 'We'll soon have you out of there,' he said. And with a wet **slop**, it was up and on its feet... or stumps. It was hard to tell either way.

Mr Blackberry waved a hand in front of his nose.

'Oooh, Arthur. I think you might need a bath in the next day or so.'

The zombie twisted and glared at Mr Blackberry. '𝐇𝐮𝐮𝐮𝐧𝐠𝐫𝐫𝐲,' it muttered.

'I'll bet you are,' said Mr Blackberry with a friendly smile. 'It can't be easy crawling up through the mud like that, certainly not for an old timer like you.'

Slowly, the creature raised its arms and staggered a small

step towards him.

Buttercup called out, 'Mr Blackberry, no!' She was about to leap towards him when the icy hand of the zombie at her feet grabbed her ankle and squeezed tight with a supernatural strength.

'Aaaghh,' she shrieked. 'Get off!' She tried to pull and kick her leg free.

'Huuungrry,' moaned Mr Blackberry's zombie, taking another shaky step.

'I'm afraid I haven't got much on me at the moment,' replied Mr Blackberry, still completely oblivious to the danger he was in. 'I can rustle up some chips back at my hut if you like.'

The thing at Buttercup's feet pulled at her leg, heaving itself further from the soil.

'Get off!' she cried, giving it another kick.

But it gripped tighter and pulled harder. 'Huungryyyyy.'

'Or I can knock up a round of sandwiches,' continued Mr Blackberry. 'Let's see, I've got jam,

Marmite, crab paste in a tiny glass jar. I've got–'

'Brains.'

'Sorry Arthur, but I don't think I've got any–'

The zombie was almost touching Mr Blackberry.

'<u>Your</u> brains.'

'Mine? What you want my brain for, you daft thing?'

Even then, poor Mr Blackberry didn't realise the very real, very horrible danger that was right in front of him. The zombie lurched forwards and clamped its hands to the side of Mr

Blackberry's head. 'Huuunngrryyy.'

Buttercup yelled, 'Mr Blackberry! That's no longer Arthur. It's the living dead. Push it away!'

But the zombie had a tight grip on Mr Blackberry and its mouth was wide open. Green slime slavered over its rotting tongue. 'Huungrryyy for brains...'

'Now, stop that. No. NO! That's cannibalism where I come from, now go on, get your hands off my aaaaahahhhhhhghhghghgh!!!'

The zombie bit down on Mr Blackberry's
head with a crunch.

Buttercup screamed,

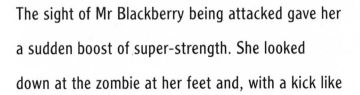

'Nooooooooo!!!'

The sight of Mr Blackberry being attacked gave her
a sudden boost of super-strength. She looked
down at the zombie at her feet and, with a kick like

a ninja, she knocked it right back into its grave. Then she ran at Mr Blackberry and shoulder charged Arthur. There was a loud **SQUELCH**. Green slime burst all over, covering Buttercup's yellow dress in globs of sticky gore as the zombie was knocked aside.

She wasted no time. She grabbed Mr Blackberry by the hand and screamed, 'Run, Mr Blackberry. We need to get out of here.'

Mr Blackberry just stood there. His eyes were open in utter disbelief. 'He bit me. That old feller bit me on the head.' And he lifted his hand to check the wound.

Buttercup was lightning fast. She grabbed Mr
Blackberry's hand and held it firm. She'd
completed a First Aid course at school and
RULE NUMBER ONE was to keep
the patient calm. If Mr Blackberry
discovered great big teeth marks in his
forehead, he'd be bound to panic.

She tried to drag him towards the gates. 'He's not
an old feller, Mr Blackberry. These things are
zombies. The walking dead. And we need to run.'

But Mr Blackberry stayed put and took a good look
around the graveyard, at the green mist, at the
figures rising to their feet, at the way their arms

stretched out in front of them and they all moaned and called out, 'Huuunngrryy.'

'Zombies?' Mr Blackberry seemed to take an age to form the words. 'But zombies aren't real. Zombies are monsters that crawl out of graves and eat brains, whereas what we have here...' he drifted off and took another look as more of the ghastly, ghoulish creatures crawled their way to the surface.

'Oh,' said Mr Blackberry. And somewhere, there was the distinct sound of a penny dropping. Mr Blackberry took a step back and said, 'I think perhaps we'd best get out of here.'

'Finally!' gasped Buttercup, pulling on his arm.

'Let's go.'

CHAPTER SEVEN

Buttercup pulled Mr Blackberry through the cemetery gates. She took another look at the gaping hole in the top of his head.

'We're going to have to get a cold compress on that,' she said. 'That's what they'd do at school.'

Secretly, she thought she'd need a whole bag of bandages to cover a wound like that but she kept

Uuuuuuugggggghhhhhhhhhhhh...   Uuuuuuugggggghhhhhhhhhh

FIRST AID WARNING SIGNS
— Nasty wound
— Sad eyes
— Lack of smile

First Aid **RULE NUMBER ONE** in mind: keep the patient calm. You go mentioning complicated procedures like bandages and they could go bananas.

'Just keep walking, Mr Blackberry.'

'Tired,' said Mr Blackberry, his eyes fluttering. 'Too tired. And I've got a terrible headache.'

'Not far to go now,' said Buttercup. This was another subtle lie. They were barely a metre from the cemetery gates.

Moans of the undead floated through the air. If

Uuuuuuugggggghhhhhhhhhh...

Uuuuuuugggggghhhhhhhh...

Buttercup wanted to save Mr Blackberry, she was going to have to deal with the zombies herself.

'Wait here,' she said. 'Wait here, Mr Blackberry. I know exactly what to do.'

*

Granny Fondant dunked a block of shortbread into her tea. 'So what did you do, my dear?'

Buttercup realised Granny wasn't keeping an eye on her shortbread and quickly called out, 'Careful Granny!'

Granny looked down, but it was too late.

The soggy biscuit snapped
and slipped into the warm tea.

'Oh, bother. This is turning into quite some day.'

'As if things couldn't get any worse,' sighed
Buttercup. She slumped back and folded her arms.
Enough was enough.

But Granny Fondant didn't panic. Very calmly, she
put her ruined tea aside and wiped her hands on
her apron. In her quiet, kindly voice she said,
'Never mind that, dear. Continue with your story.
How did you help Mr Blackberry?'

Buttercup huffed, shuffled into a more comfy position and tried again. 'Well, with Mr Blackberry being all dizzy and wobbly, I knew he'd never make it to his hut with all those zombies following. I could hear them groaning and staggering about in the cemetery, calling out for our brains and whatnot. It was only a matter of time before they found us. We couldn't run, and with Mr Blackberry barely able to walk, we couldn't stand and fight either.'

'So what did you do?'

'Well. That's when I remembered the booklets Miss Morbid gave us. They looked a bit homemade to be

honest and she didn't half hand them out in a
hurry. Booklets on all kinds of things. Let me think.
There was...'

'Just tell me about the one that helped you.'

'Oh, that! It was called "Run! Zombies are

coming." Then it had a

smaller title below,

something about

being an essential

guide for children.

Inside, it had

information on

how to spot a

zombie, how to evade capture and how to stop them. And the only sure way to stop them eating your brain is to destroy the *zombie*'s brain. Clever, eh? So I thought, how am I, a little girl without so much as a pointed stick, going to do that?'

Zombie brain

Granny Fondant's eyes shifted to the chainsaw on the carpet. 'You went back to the bonfire?'

Buttercup beamed. 'I did! I ran back, and I grabbed the chainsaw.'

*

Buttercup didn't realise just how heavy that chainsaw was until she tried to pick it up. It weighed a ton. But in times of need, people can find an inner strength and that's exactly what Buttercup Sunshine found. She held the machine in both hands and ran and ran and ran.

By the time she had returned to Mr Blackberry, he was staggering all over the place. He was bouncing off the trees and he looked terrible. His eyes were red, his cheeks were sunken and his skin had a horrible tinge of green. To make things worse, the zombies had found their way through the cemetery gates and were shambling their way towards him.

Buttercup ran forward. 'Watch out, Mr Blackberry.'

She put herself between the wobbly lumberjack and the zombies. Then she held the chainsaw firm and pulled hard on the starter cord.

The engine turned over, there was a roar, then a splutter, a cough and the engine died. She tried again and exactly the same thing happened. And the zombies were coming closer.

'Mr Blackberry! What's wrong?'

Mr Blackberry's reply was a moan. There was something about that moan that made Buttercup uncomfortable. 'Mr Blackberry?'

The lumberjack didn't answer. Instead, he staggered about another few paces, then he slowly raised his arms and his eyes locked onto Buttercup.

'Huuunngry,' he moaned.

'Hungry for...'

'Oh, heck,' whispered Buttercup.

*

'And then what did you do?' asked Granny.

'Well I didn't hang about, did I? I remembered two important things. First, the booklet said that if you get bitten by a zombie, you turn into one too – no matter how small the wound. And second, Mr Blackberry had said his chainsaw drank petrol in five minutes flat, so I realised it must be empty. I thought he'd have some more back at his hut. Makes sense, right? So that's what I did. I ran right back to his hut and had a good look around. But no petrol. He'd used it all up. By the time I'd finished looking and stepped outside, there was Mr Blackberry with

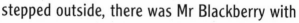

AN ENTIRE ARMY OF ZOMBIES

behind him.' Buttercup leaned forward. 'They were sniffing the air, Granny. They could smell my brains. And unless I got some petrol soon, nothing was going to stop them.'

'So you came here? But I don't have any petrol. I already told you, I don't even have a car.'

Buttercup craned her neck to look through the window. The zombies were close. Very, very close.

'I didn't come just for petrol, Granny. The zombies were going to follow me, no matter what. So I had a choice, see? Lead them to the town where they

can feed on all our friends and family, or come and find my Granny. Because I believe in you, Granny. Together, we can think of a plan to defeat the hordes of the undead and save our town!'

Buttercup shot to her feet, standing right in the middle of the front room like a warrior. 'What do you think, Granny? Are you up for it? Are you ready to stand shoulder to shoulder and battle the undead?'

Warrior pose →

A low scrape on the wood of the garden gate

announced the arrival of the mass of zombies.

Granny Fondant slapped her hands on her knees.

'So they want brains, do they?' The old lady's

eyes narrowed and a sly smile spread on Granny's

wrinkled lips.

'Then that's exactly what we'll give them.'

sly smile

CHAPTER EIGHT

Buttercup thought she'd explode with joy. 'I *knew* you'd have a plan, Granny. I just knew it. I *knew* it. So what is it? What are we gonna do?'

Granny gave the little girl a wink, reached forward and picked up two of her longest knitting needles.

Buttercup's eyes widened. 'You're not planning on going out there, are you? You're not going to use those knitting needles as weapons and go head to head with the army of the undead?'

'No, dear. I'm going to knit.'

'But Granny, this is no time for knitting. We need action, not a cardigan.'

Granny grinned, showing the tops of her false teeth and clicked the ends of the needles together. 'Oh, I'm not planning on knitting a cardigan, Buttercup.'

'No? Then what?'

'A scarf.'

'A scarf?' Buttercup was shocked. 'It's not even snowing.'

'This isn't to keep us warm, dear. Now, no more arguments. What I need is some red wool, some pink, some grey and some green. Also some white.' She frowned, thinking through her plan. 'And some blue. Hand me that bag over there with all my spare ends. I should have just about enough to make this work.'

As Buttercup reached for the bag, Granny quickly explained her idea.

'That's a fantastic plan,' cried Buttercup. 'It's incredible. It's amazing. But will we have time?'

'I don't know, dear. I've never knitted under such pressure.'

BANG!

A loud bang from the front door made Buttercup jump. It was enough to snap her mind back to the job in hand. If Granny was knitting, Buttercup had other work to do.

'While you work on the scarf, I'll secure the entry

points.'

Oh, if only she had Barry to keep in touch from his operations centre. Thinking of her partner suddenly gave Buttercup a brilliant idea. She thrust a hand into the pocket of her dress and pulled out the two tiny earpieces. She picked off bits of yellow fluff and handed one to Granny.

'We can stay in contact with these.' She placed the second earpiece in her own ear. 'Micro walkie-talkies,' she explained. 'An active range of up to fifty metres.'

'Can't we just shout?'

'You're no spring chicken, Granny. The last thing we need is for you to wear yourself out shouting.' Her face was deadly serious. 'You've got knitting to do.'

There was another loud BANG on the front door.

Granny pulled out a large ball of grey wool. 'Perfect.' And with a loud double-click, she loaded her knitting needles. 'Let's go knit some butt!'

CHAPTER NINE

Buttercup went directly to the pantry. The pantry was by the back door and, as well as being a larder filled with dried and canned foods, it also doubled up as a garden shed. Granny's purple wellies were by the back door next to a garden rake, a spade and a small lawnmower. There was a workbench too. This hadn't been used since Grandpa was around, and now it was covered in all kinds of rubbish, but there, underneath, was a toolbox.

Buttercup dropped to her knees and pulled the box towards her. Inside she found a hammer and a bag of six-inch nails.

'Just what I need.'

She was about to push the toolbox back but something right at the back caught her eye. 'Is that what I think it is?' She reached in and pulled out Grandpa's old leather tool-belt. The buckle was slightly rusty, the tan leather was crisscrossed with creases and scars but the utility pockets felt solid.

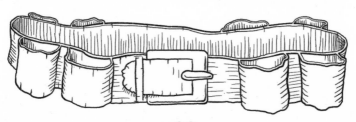

'Even better.'

She attached the belt, pulled it tight and fixed the bag of nails to the back. She slotted the hammer into a pocket on the right, checked it was sturdy then ran to the front door. She whipped out a six-inch nail, held it in place and gave it a good, hard whack with the hammer.

BANG!

The nail was driven deep into the wood of the door.

Oh, that felt good.

BANG, BANG, BANG!

She pulled out another nail and did the same
again, driving nails through the edge of the door,
straight into the frame and effectively locking it
tight.

'Front door secured,' she called.

In her ear, Granny's voice came back: 'We've got

two of those zombies approaching the living room windows.'

'Copy that,' replied Buttercup. 'I'm on it now.'

Buttercup ran into the front room and vaulted over the back of the sofa. As she somersaulted through the air she pulled out a nail and whacked it home as she landed.

BANG!

The grim faces of the undead barely reacted to the sound. They just stared in, their eyes fixed on Buttercup as they moaned in their inhuman tones, 'Braaaiiinsss.'

Buttercup ignored them and hammered nails into the window frames.

BANG, BANG, BANG!

'The area is secured. You keep working, Granny. I'll

check the rear entrance.'

'That's a ten-four, dear.'

Buttercup returned to the pantry and secured the back door. Then she did the same with the window that looked onto the back garden. The kitchen was next, followed by every other window on the ground floor.

'Are you doing the upstairs too?' asked Granny.

Buttercup glanced up the stairs. 'I don't think zombies can climb the drain pipes. We should be okay.' She walked back into the front room. 'How's the scarf going?'

But she could see exactly how it was going and her heart sank.

Granny looked up, her face dark with apology. 'I'm afraid it's early days yet. This may take some time.'

A sudden **CRASH** from the windows shot a bolt of panic right down Buttercup's spine. Glass showered the room as dark green hands pushed through.

'They've smashed the glass!'

'We're going to need a glazier.'

'We need more than that. They'll be inside the cottage before we know it.' Buttercup needed something to fend them off. She needed something to throw.

The bookshelves! Granny was a great fan of romantic fiction and those shelves were absolutely crammed with paperbacks.

Buttercup grabbed a handful and began throwing the books at the living dead. 'Get back!' she called. But the books spun and fluttered

open. Half of them didn't even reach the zombies.
There must be a better way to chuck a book.

Two zombies were now leaning in through the
broken glass.

'Braiiinnnnnssss.'

'Don't give me any of that,' she called and grabbed
more books. 'Get out of my Granny's window.' She
held the next book flat on her palm and flung the
thing like a custard pie. The book sailed through
the air, the pages kept tight shut and the book

slapped the first zombie smack in the face. But other than that, it didn't really inflict any damage at all.

She dumped the rest of the books on the floor with a cry of, 'Oh, this is useless.'

She looked round. To the right of the shelves was a large lamp stand.

'That'll do.' She grabbed the stand and ripped the cable from the wall. Then, using the stand as some kind of spear with a large lampshade attached, Buttercup jabbed at the zombies, and she kept

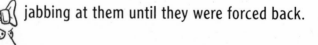 jabbing at them until they were forced back.

She dumped the lamp stand on the floor. 'I've held them back, but it's not going to stop them.' She noticed that Granny was watching, her ancient eyes brimming with concern.

'Don't worry, Granny. You keep working on the scarf. I'll deal with the undead.'

A second later, Buttercup was back in the pantry, searching through the toolbox, looking here and there and...

'Aha! A crowbar. Perfect.'

This was a large metal bar with a hook at one end

and a sharp flat point at the other. She grabbed it, ran back to the front room and jammed the tip of the crowbar under the empty bookshelves. In one quick movement, she ripped the shelves from the wall.

At the window, the zombies were leaning back inside the cottage.

Buttercup gave them a sharp jab with the shelf and the moment they moved back she placed it against the window frame.

She grabbed a nail and pulled out her hammer.

BANG!

Another nail.

BANG!

And another.

BANG,
BANG,
BANG!

The window was barred shut with two solid

shelves. The zombies clawed their hands through the gaps, but could do no more.

'That should hold them for a while,' said Buttercup.

Granny didn't look up. She was clicking those needles like a machine gun. 'Do the dining room and kitchen,' she said. 'Plenty more shelves upstairs.'

Granny was right. Up in the spare room, every inch of wall space was covered in shelves, and the shelves were packed with hundreds of floppy paperbacks.

Buttercup tore down the books, making a mountain of weepy fiction. Then she jammed the crowbar in place and ripped that room to pieces.

Downstairs. Hammer. Nails.

BANG!
BANG, BANG, BANG!

'Dining room secure.'

BANG, BANG, BANG!

'Kitchen secure. How's the scarf going, Granny?'

'We've got a problem, honey. Actually, we've got two.'

Buttercup ran into the front room, and she immediately saw the first problem for herself.

When she was last in here, there were only a couple of hands reaching in through the wooden window barricades. Now, there were loads. Every single space had an arm or a hand or a head pushing through.

'There are too many,' said Granny. 'Those boards will never hold.'

As if on cue, one of the shelves suddenly cracked and splintered.

Buttercup jumped at the sound. 'I'll need to find some ingenious way of holding them back.' She turned round to face Granny. 'What's the other problem?'

The old lady's face was grim. 'I've run out of pink wool.'

CHAPTER TEN

Quick as a flash, Buttercup raced upstairs. There was a large, crochet blanket on the bed – and the bulk of the pattern was pink. She grabbed it, ran downstairs and threw it at Granny. 'Can you deconstruct this?'

Granny snipped the end with a pair of scissors. 'Already on it. But we still need to deal with the zombies at the windows. If you don't find a way to

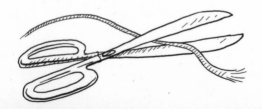

hold them back, all of this knitting will be for
nothing.'

'No, Granny, no! I will not have you knit in vain!'
She looked around. 'I need a cordless vacuum
cleaner and a long hose.'

'The vacuum cleaner is on charge under the stairs.
There's a coil of hose by the back door. What's
your plan, deary?'

'No time to explain, Granny. I can do, or I can
teach.'

'Then you better just do what you need to do,

Buttercup.'

Buttercup ran back to the pantry and searched through the tool box. Using the micro walkie-talkie in her ear, she gave Granny an update on her progress. 'I've got a screwdriver and a pair of pliers but what I really need is... Yes! Extra-strong duct tape. Perfect.'

A moment later, she was thumping her way upstairs with the hose under one arm, the vacuum cleaner under the other and everything else fitted snugly in her tool-belt.

She attached the hose to the bath tap and taped it

up tight, giving it a quick tug to check it was fixed. Next, she began pulling the vacuum cleaner apart.

'If I can rewire it to blow instead of suck...' Her words drifted off as she concentrated on the task in hand. Red wire. Blue wire. Snip, strip and re-attach. It was times like this she was glad she had paid attention in Miss Morbid's engineering class.

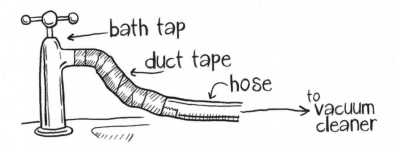

bath tap

duct tape

hose

to vacuum cleaner

'I've reversed the polarity on the motor,' she called. 'Give me a status update on the scarf, Granny.'

'Deconstruction of the blanket underway. Another thirty seconds and I can return to the main task.'

'Keep going. I've connected the hose to the pipe of the vacuum cleaner. Time to see if the seal is watertight.'

Buttercup turned the cold tap on full power. Water began to pour from the business end of the vacuum cleaner. 'That's a ten-four on the seal, Granny. Time to take this baby to the roof.'

'Be careful up there, Buttercup. If you slip and fall, you'll land in the garden. The last thing you need is mud on that dress as well as zombie slime.'

'It's okay, Granny.

This dress is stain resistant polyester.

One quick wash and it'll be as good as new.'

Buttercup opened the upstairs window and with
the vacuum cleaner slung over her shoulder and
water pouring behind her, she climbed out through
the window onto the thatched roof of the cottage.

She took a firm stand, looked down at the hordes
of the undead and called out, 'Get your rotting
hands off my Granny's cottage.'

At the sound of her voice, several zombies
stretched their hands up towards her, and as a

mass they called out, 'Braaaaiiiinnnsss.'

Granny's voice crackled through the earpiece.
'What have you made, dear?'

Buttercup didn't take her eyes off the zombies
below. 'A water cannon.' Then she clenched her
teeth tight and clicked the power switch and
turned her machine on.

The combined pressure of compressed air and
flowing water was explosive. Water shot out of the
end of the vacuum with such power that Buttercup
had to dig her heels into the thatched roof and
lean hard against her creation just to remain

standing.

She screamed against the noise of the blast and
aimed directly at the zombies below. They didn't
stand a chance. The blast hit them like a watery
train, knocking them back from the house.

'It's working,' she called. 'It's working, Granny.'
And then she screamed out, 'Take that, you rotting
monsters. It's payback time.'

CHAPTER ELEVEN

Buttercup continued blasting the zombies with her homemade water cannon. But as soon as she moved from the front of the house to the back, the zombies she had turned away from began to push back towards the cottage.

The plan was failing.

'There are too many, Granny. I can't hold them all

back. How long until scarf completion?'

Granny's voice replied through her earpiece, 'E.T.A. two minutes and fifteen seconds.'

'What's the hold up?' She returned to the front of the house and blasted the zombies below.

'I just need to cast off and double stitch to avoid fraying at the edges,' replied Granny.

'Don't worry about fraying, Granny. We need that scarf now!'

There was a sudden **CRASH** from the back

of the house. Buttercup ran across the roof and looked down. Her eyes almost popped. One of the zombies was head and shoulders into the property.

'Noooooooo!!!'

Buttercup aimed the water cannon directly down. But the whole mob of zombies were pushing forward and, before the blast could hit them, the zombie leaning in through the broken window was pushed inside.

Buttercup pressed her walkie-talkie hard against her ear and called out, 'Granny, be advised! We've got a break in at the rear of the building.'

'What's that?'

'The perimeter is compromised, Granny. We've got hostiles in the building. Repeat, hostiles in the building. Prepare to engage.'

Buttercup dropped the water cannon where it was, ran back to the open bedroom window and dived inside.

The shortest distance between two points is a straight line, so rather than run around the bed, Buttercup jumped right over. She landed, hoping to bounce herself right through the door.

But Granny's bed was super soft, and the blankets that covered the duvet were deep and thick. It was like landing in quicksand. The blankets and duvet wrapped around her ankles like a woolly bear-trap.

Buttercup fell forward on the bed.

'No!' She kicked her legs, but it only seemed to make the blankets wrap tighter.

'Granny,' she called. 'I'm trapped. You need to get out of there.'

'Almost done, dear. Just finishing off now.'

Panic gripped Buttercup like a claw. Granny clearly didn't grasp the imminent danger. So she kicked and writhed and twisted and finally managed to tear herself away from the bed. And with a thump, she landed on the bedroom floor.

Buttercup didn't waste any more time. She jumped

to her feet and raced to the hallway. As she got to the top of the stairs, she looked down to see that single zombie shuffling its way into the front room.

'Grannneee!'

Buttercup threw herself down the stairs, landing heavily at the bottom and burst into the front room.

But it was too late.

CHAPTER TWELVE

The entire, horribly grotesque scene happened in a flash before Buttercup could do a thing.

Granny Fondant was on her feet. The scarf had slipped from her needles and the zombie had its hands clamped onto Granny's head.

'Braaaiiinnsss.'

Its jaws were open.

Granny screamed.

The zombie leaned forward and prepared to bite.

Buttercup leapt forward and jumped on the creature's back. She kicked and punched and grabbed and yanked, pulling the foul creature away from her beloved Granny.

And then... the zombie slumped to the floor.
Buttercup stepped back, puzzled for a moment.
That's when she saw the knitting needles, with
green slime dripping from them, and she gasped at
what Granny had done.

'Destroy the brain,' said Granny. 'Just like
you said.' Then she fell back into her chair.
'The scarf is ready to go.'

With horror, Buttercup noticed a row of teeth-
marks in Granny Fondant's forehead. She
thought she'd pulled the creature away in
time. She thought Granny had been spared.

All she could say was, 'Granny. You're hurt.'

'I'm okay, dear. But that was a little too close for comfort. You need to fix the window he came through. Nail it shut, just like before, then get the scarf in position.'

All Buttercup could think about were the words in that booklet: no matter how small the wound.

'But Granny, you're *hurt!*'

Granny grabbed Buttercup's arms and gave her a firm shake. 'The window. Fix it now. Then get that scarf out there.'

Her grip relaxed. She slipped back into her chair and her eyes closed. 'I'm okay, dear. I'm okay. Just go. Keep them out.'

Buttercup ran to the pantry. There were other zombies leaning in through the broken window and shattered boards, but they were so tightly packed that none could actually climb inside.

She grabbed a spare shelf and hammered it across the gap. With a tear in her eye, she called out, 'Stay out of my Granny's house!'

She ran back to the front room. The scarf was on the floor in a pile and Granny appeared to be

asleep.

'Granny?'

'Just resting my eyes, dear. It's been a busy morning. Take the scarf. Go.'

Without another word, Buttercup ran for the stairs with the scarf in hand. But in her ear, she could hear Granny quietly moaning, 'Oh no. Oh, deary no, no, no.'

CHAPTER THIRTEEN

Buttercup climbed back up onto the roof. The zombies were hammering at the boarded-up doors and she knew they wouldn't hold out more than just a few seconds. It was now or never.

She quickly tied the loose ends of the scarf to the edge of the cottage roof, one at that end, then running back across the roof to fix the other to this end.

'It's all in place, Granny. Shall I let it go?'

'Whenever you're ready,' came the tired reply. 'Let them have it.'

Buttercup unravelled the scarf and let it tumble down, and as it did she very nearly collapsed with pride at what Granny had created. This wasn't a simple scarf with a colourful design. This was a banner. The colours were stunning, the lettering perfectly clear, even the image of a brain on a plate was perfect.

What's more, it had the zombies' attention. They were staring up at the giant image of a brain and raising their hands. 'Braaiinss.'

'What if they can't read the words?' said
Buttercup.

'You only need one,' whispered Granny. 'As soon as
one makes that connection, the rest will fall like
dominoes.'

And there, down on the lawn, head and shoulders
above the others, Buttercup could make out Mr
Blackberry, the lumberjack. He was squinting at
the sign and muttering something.

'Go on,' said Buttercup. 'You can do it, Mr Blackberry. You've only been undead for a matter of hours. The human part of your brain is still working. Just read the words, Mr Blackberry. Read the words...'

Slowly, Mr Blackberry's finger began to rise and point. 'Braaiinnss,' he called, just like the others. 'Braaainsss.'

'It's not working, Granny.'

Granny's voice was quieter than ever, 'We gave it our best shot, dear. That's all we could do.'

Buttercup stared at Mr Blackberry, willing him to make the connection. 'Read the words, Mr Blackberry, just read the words.'

Mr Blackberry moaned and swayed, his eyes trying to focus.

The other zombies cried out, 'Braaiinnns,' but Mr Blackberry was quiet, just swaying and staring at the huge letters on the banner.

'Go on,' whispered Buttercup. 'Go on, Mr Blackberry.'

The lumberjack's lips began to wobble. He was

forming what looked like words.

'Go on,' called Buttercup.

And then came his voice, rasping and gravelly,
'*All...*'

'Yes! Go on, Mr Blackberry. Read the words.'

'*All...*'

'Yes!'

'*All you can...*'

'That's it, Mr Blackberry. Read the words. You can do it!'

'All you can eat.'

And suddenly, the moans of all the other zombies stopped. As a mass, they looked at Mr Blackberry. Mr Blackberry continued to stare upwards.

This time, he read all the words on the banner.

'BRAINS...' he seemed to stumble over the second word. 'B... BANQUET. ALL YOU CAN EAT.'

BRAINS BANQUET ALL YOU CAN EAT!

Knitted into the scarf were huge arrows and a picture of the gates of the Forgotten Cemetery, just as Buttercup had described them to Granny.

All the zombies were staring in silence at Mr Blackberry who slowly turned and pointed back the way they'd come.

'BRAAINSSSS,' he called. 'Brains b...banquet.'

dinner

He began to shuffle towards the gate. 'All you can eaaaaat!'

Buttercup punched the air. 'Yes! It's working, Granny. The legion of the undead is retreating. They're heading back to the forest, back to the Wicked Woods of Woe. They're leaving, Granny. The scarf did the trick. You're a genius.'

Having no reply, Buttercup climbed back in through the window. Her feet were heavy from exhaustion, but she clambered downstairs, driven on by a desperate need to see her beloved Granny Fondant and tell her that the plan had worked.

CHAPTER FOURTEEN

Buttercup staggered into the room ready to drop. The whole night finally hit home in a wave of exhaustion. Everything from spotting the star and finding the cemetery to boarding up the windows, making a water cannon and unveiling the banner.

'We did it, Granny,' she said. 'We beat them. They're retreating.'

Granny sat in the chair, her breathing shallow. Her head was down and she looked almost asleep. In a quiet sleepy hiss, she said, 'Retreating, dear?'

'Mr Blackberry's leading them back to the Forgotten Cemetery. By time they realise the brains banquet doesn't exist, we'll be ready to regroup and start a counter attack. I'll go the store and stock up on weapons. But we need to move.' She paused. 'Are you okay Granny?'

'Just tired, dear. All of this excitement has been...' She drifted off, her head lolling to one side. Her breathing, once again, was laboured.

'Granny?' A strange feeling stirred in Buttercup's stomach. Something wasn't right. 'Granny? Shall I put the kettle on? It's been a bit of a morning, perhaps a nice cup of tea...'

Granny continued to breathe slowly, her breaths beginning to rasp in the back of her throat. She muttered something, but the words were little more than a moan.

'Granny? Are you feeling okay? You look terribly pale.'

Granny's words were little more than a growl.

Buttercup stepped closer. 'What was that, Granny? I can't quite hear you.'

'Hungry,' moaned Granny.

That feeling in Buttercup's stomach continued to grow. She noticed that the line of teeth marks on Granny's forehead were blackened and swollen. And once again, she recalled the words from Miss Morbid's booklet: no matter how small the wound.

'Huuuunngry.'

Buttercup chose her words carefully. 'I think we

finished off the rest of the shortbread earlier.'

'Don't want shhhhhhort brrread,'
whispered Granny. 'Hunnngry...'

Buttercup swallowed, suddenly realising that the
windows and doors were still boarded up. 'Then,
perhaps a biscuit?'

'Don't waaaannnnt
bissssCuits,' moaned Granny.

Her fingers clawed the edges of the chair and her
head slowly rose up. Her skin had a deathly green
tinge, slime drooled from her dry lips and her eyes

Big zombie bite mark →

Eyes lost their sparkle

A bit dribbly →

← Lack of smile

were blood red with piercing black dots.

Buttercup took a nervous step backwards.

'Hungry,' moaned Granny, stretching out her hands and slowly clawing at the air.

'Hungry

for...

your...

BRAAIIIINNS!'

Buttercup took another step back, shaking her head. 'Oh no. No, Granny. I can't have this. You can't be one of the walking dead.'

Granny shuffled forward. 'Braaaiinnss.'

'That wound is barely a scratch.'

'Hunnnnnnnngry.'

Buttercup blinked her tears away and wiped her eyes with the back of her hand.

Granny just stood there, waving her clawed hands as she slowly advanced.

But Buttercup wasn't afraid. Instead, her brain was racing, and in a second she knew exactly what to do. She kept her eyes on Granny and said, 'Miss Morbid seemed to know this was coming, so maybe she knows how to help you.' She took another step back, keeping her distance. 'That's what I'm going to do, Granny. I'm going back to school right now and I'm going to fix this. You see if I don't.'

Buttercup Sunshine left Granny's house, kicked open the garden gate and ran out onto Honeysuckle Lane. She ran and she ran, heading for the little town of Briar's Cove – the nicest, safest, sweetest town there ever was.

Where nothing bad ever happens...

...until now.

Keep an eye out for Buttercup's
next adventure, coming soon:

Buttercup Sunshine

AND THE

HOUSE ON HANGMAN'S HILL

ABOUT THE AUTHOR

Colin has always had a love of writing, submitting his first manuscript when he was just thirteen years old. As well as working in the video games industry as an artist and designer for eight years, he currently works as a teaching assistant in a primary school and has a huge passion for making people laugh. *Buttercup Sunshine and the Zombies of Dooooom* was inspired by his eldest son,

Matthew, and Colin knew he wanted to write something exciting, fast-paced and very, very silly.

We asked Colin some very important questions:

What's your favourite colour?
Cerulean.

If you had three wishes what would they be?
To find a working time machine, to discover
interstellar travel and meet a few alien races and
to play the drums like Charlie Benante.

What's your favourite type of dinosaur?
The Loch Ness Monster.

If you had a super power what would it be?
How about being able to sneeze with your eyes
open – that's the sort of talent that can get you on
TV these days.

28·9·8·

MALPAS
REVIEWS FOR
BUTTERCUP

"Think **SCOOBY-DOO** - comedy-horror and a young detective. This is **HILARIOUS!**"
Book Murmuration

"This is a **LIVELY** and **UNUSUAL** story for children of 7+ who want some gentle scaring along with plenty of humour."
Parents in Touch

"Turn off the lights, grab yourself a torch, pull the bedcovers over your head and settle down for **LAUGHS** and **CHILL-THRILLS**."
The Letterpress Project